# Yes

The Story of a Dreamer

By Frankie Ann Marcille

Illustrated by Patrick Regan

Leaning Rock Press

Leaning Rock Press, LLC
Gales Ferry, CT 06335
leaningrockpress@gmail.com
www.leaningrockpress.com

978-1-950323-35-7, Hardcover
978-1-950323-38-8, Softcover

Library of Congress Control Number: 2021901130

Publisher's Cataloging-In-Publication Data
(Prepared by The Donohue Group, Inc.)

Names: Marcille, Frankie Ann, author. | Regan, Patrick, 1994- illustrator.
Title: "Yes" : the story of a dreamer / by Frankie Ann Marcille ; i
    llustrated by Patrick Regan.
Description: Gales Ferry, CT : Leaning Rock Press, [2021] | Interest age
    level: 006-012. | Summary: "When the author was a little girl, she had
    many wonderful dreams. As she began to share her hopes and dreams, she
    noticed something that made her heart sink. People began to tell her,
    "No, you can't do those things. You can't because you can't see." This
    is a story, based on her life, about meeting a person who finally told
    her, 'Yes, you can do whatever you put your mind to.' And she did
    exactly that."--Provided by publisher.
Identifiers: ISBN 9781950323357 (hardcover) | ISBN 9781950323388
    (softcover)
Subjects: LCSH: People with visual disabilities--Psychology--Juvenile
    literature. | Marcille, Frankie Ann--Juvenile literature. | Self-
    actualization (Psychology)--Juvenile literature. | Ambition--Juvenile
    literature. | Encouragement--Juvenile literature. | CYAC: People with
    visual disabilities--Psychology. | Marcille, Frankie Ann. | Self-
    actualization (Psychology) | Ambition. | Encouragement.
Classification: LCC HV1593 .M37 2021 | DDC 362.41--dc23

Published in the United States of America

For S.M. and F.M.~
The first people to tell me "Yes".
You mean everything to me.
I'll love you forever.

For D.N.~
My Gardener.
I never got the chance to tell you:
I would not be where I am today if not for you.

For all of the other "Gardeners" in my life~
Thank you for pushing me
To get on that dance floor,
To say yes to that lead role,
To write that paper, poem, or play,
To paint that tablecloth,
To come to "blind camp".
Thank you for filling my life with dreams,
my sky with stars.

For J.W.O.~
With you, I see the stars reflecting
from a galaxy far, far away.
I love you to Edinburgh and beyond.

When I was a little girl, I would lay in the dark before bed.
When I fell asleep,
I had many wonderful dreams that made the darkness a little brighter,
like twinkling lights on a Christmas tree.

I dreamt of dancing across glorious stages in front of crowds of people,
bringing joy to their hearts and smiles to their faces.
I dreamt of being expressive and free.

**I dreamt of dancing.**

I dreamt of traveling the world,
crossing deep blue oceans, and climbing mountains that seemed to graze the heavens.
I dreamt of the various cultures, sights, and sounds each unique location offered.

**I dreamt of traveling.**

I dreamt of becoming a teacher,
sharing my experiences with the next generation of dreamers.
I dreamt of changing lives, one student at a time.

**I dreamt of teaching.**

4

When I was a little girl, after a night of dreaming,
I would spring from my bed, excited to share my dreams.
But, I noticed something that made my heart sink.
People began to frown. People exchanged worried glances.

**People told me, "No."**

**"You're different," they said.**

"How can you dance on stage if you can't see in the lights?"
"How can you find your way backstage in the dark?"
"How can you turn without falling?"

**"You can't be a dancer because you can't see."**

**"You're different," they said.**

"How can you travel if you can't drive a car?"
"How can you get on a plane if you can't read the signs?"
"How can you find your way in a new place if you can't cross the street?"

**"You can't travel the world because you can't see."**

**"You're different," they said.**

"How can you be a teacher if you can't see the back row of desks in a classroom?"
"How can you be responsible for children when you can't focus on the entire room?"
"How can you show your students examples if you can't read the small print?"

**"You can't be a teacher because you can't see."**

One night, when it was time for bed, I curled up in my blankets, ready to fall asleep.
My mother kissed me goodnight and turned off the light.
My room had never felt so dark before.
A tear rolled down my cheek and across my pillow. I tried with all of my strength to fall asleep.
And for the first time, I had no dreams at all.

**Then, one day I met a man.**

He was tall with white hair and bright blue eyes that twinkled behind his glasses.
On his hands, he wore withered gloves, and on his shoulder, he carried a large bag.

He was different from anyone I had ever known.
He was kind.
He was warm,
and he smiled at me.

11

"I am the Gardener, " he said.
"Planter of dreams, keeper of the stars.
Now tell me, little one, what are your dreams?"
I stared at the man and then, looking down at my feet,
I said quietly, "I don't have any."

12

The man laughed. I looked back up at him and saw his smile had widened.
"Oh, that's silly!" he chuckled.
"You must have a dream! Everyone has at least one!
And I want to hear all about yours."

13

I felt my heart fluttering in my chest.
My eyes came alive as I began to tell this wonderful man all about my dreams.

I told him about dancing, and traveling, and teaching.
I told him about glorious stages, deep oceans, and mountains that grazed the heavens.
I told him about the next generation of dreamers.

I told him about all of the people I wanted to meet,
and help, and work with to change the world.
I told him everything.
The man listened quietly, his gaze never leaving mine.

When I had finished, the man put his hand on my shoulder.
"You are quite the dreamer," he said.

My gaze shifted down to my feet.
"I used to be," I whispered. "But I can't do any of these things because I can't see."
For the first time since I met him, the old man frowned.
"Who told you that?" He asked.
"Everyone," I answered.

"Can I tell you a secret?" he asked, leaning in close to me.
As I nodded slowly, the man reached into his bag, pulled something out, and placed it in my hand.
It was a small ball of light that gleamed in my palm.

**"They're wrong," he said.**

"What is it?" I asked in amazement.
"That," said the man, "is a star."

I had never seen a star before.
I had only pictured them in my dreams.
I sat mesmerized, watching its light dance across my fingers.
And as I held this beautiful star, I felt my heart begin to beat faster and faster.

"Stars are the seeds that allow dreams to grow," the man said.
"You are a dreamer and this star now belongs to you.
Someone, who dreams as much as you do, can do anything.
I am here to tell you, '**Yes**, you can do anything!'
Just keep on dreaming and let your star shine bright."
I smiled at the man.
"Thank you," I said before placing the star in my own pocket.

21

The next night, when the sun had faded, and it was time for bed,
I curled up in my blankets ready to fall asleep.
My mother kissed me goodnight and turned off the light.

**Only this time, something was different.**

I leapt out of bed and ran to pull my star out of my pocket,
marveling at the wonderful thing I had in my hand.
I held the star to my heart for a moment before putting it under my pillow.
I closed my eyes.
That night I had the most amazing dream of all.

In the dream, I was a grown-up, living in an incredible city.
I danced across many glorious stages for crowds of people.
I traveled the world, crossing deep blue oceans and climbing mountains.
I was a teacher, sharing my experiences with the next generation of dreamers.
I did everything I ever wanted to do.

**And I was very happy.**

That was long ago when I was a little girl. Now, I am a grown-up.

I live in an amazing city.
I have danced.
I have traveled.
I have taught.

I am happier than I ever dreamed I could be,
all because one man told me,

**"Yes."**

Last night I had a new dream.
I was sitting with a young girl.
She was crying because no one believed in her.
Everyone was telling her, "**No.**"

Pulling her close, I dried her eyes,
reached into my pocket and dropped something in her hand.
It was that same star that the kind man had given to me many years ago.
The young girl looked at me with puzzled eyes.

**"They're wrong," I said to her.**

"That is a star.
Stars are the seeds that allow dreams to grow.
You are a dreamer and this star now belongs to you.
Someone, who dreams as much as you do, can do anything.
I am here to tell you, '**Yes**, you can do anything!'
Just keep on dreaming and let your star shine bright."

29

The young girl held the star in her palm
and watched as its light danced across her fingers.
Pulling the star close to her heart, her eyes met mine
as she smiled and mouthed one simple word.

YES

# Author
# Frankie Ann Marcille

**Frankie Ann Marcille** is a legally blind author, educator, and advocate from southeastern Connecticut, currently residing in Manhattan, New York. At three months old, she was diagnosed with septo-optic dysplasia; a condition that resulted in legal blindness. Frankie Ann has spent her entire life adapting to her visual impairment, learning to never let it hold her back, and advocating for others to do the same! She earned her BA in Theatre Arts from Western Connecticut State University and is currently studying to obtain her M.Ed. in Vision Rehabilitation Therapy/Orientation and Mobility from Hunter College.

Over the past decade, Frankie Ann has traveled the country, teaching and advocating for individuals of all ages with multiple disabilities. Most recently, she has been working as a Mentor and Teacher for two of the Utah School for the Deaf and Blind's virtual learning programs. She has recently joined the team at Elle Jones Casting Company; representing and advocating for accessibility for disabled actors.

When she's not advocating, Frankie Ann enjoys going on adventures with her boyfriend, Jim, spending a weekend at the beach with her family, hiking, dancing, reading, and of course... writing! She is a contributing writer for blogs such as "Paths to Technology" (run by the Perkins School for the Blind), "Anxiously Blogging" (testimonials on living with anxiety, run by Mareena Bartelli), and "Chickadee Collective" (a resource for female artists who want to take control of their careers, run by Tara Llewellyn). She also runs her own advocacy/accessibility blog called "Blind Ambition". Frankie Ann could not be more excited to be fulfilling her lifelong dream of being an author and sharing her story with you!

**To learn more about Frankie Ann, please visit:**
**frankieannmarcille.com**

# Illustrator
# Patrick Regan

**Patrick Regan** is an illustrator, graphic, and motion graphic designer from New London, Connecticut. He had an ambitious and creative drive from an early age. Growing up, Patrick was inspired by Star Wars, The Lord of the Rings, and Batman. He spent countless hours at the kitchen table bringing his imagination to life, and in doing so, he created and destroyed hundreds of fictional characters and universes.

Ultimately, this led to his enrollment at the Hartford Art School, where he began to refine his skills. He received a BFA in illustration in 2016. Since graduating, Patrick has worked full time as an in-house motion graphic designer for Astor Place, Inc, a video production and marketing company. He also has worked on hundreds of freelance illustration and design projects, including book cover art, beer can art, T-shirt designs, album art, logo designs, book layouts and illustrations, concept art, tattoos, private commissions, and more.

When not working on commissioned projects, Patrick is busy designing, illustrating, animating, and bringing to life his own fantasy world projects. He enjoys collecting comics and vinyl, reading, and spending time at the beach.

**Patrick can be reached at:**
**patrick_regan@sbcglobal.net**

**His portfolio can be viewed at:**
**faireharbourart.com**

# A Note from the Author

"Yes" and "No". Two of the simplest, shortest, but most powerful words. One has the power to lift a person up; to motivate them to achieve their dreams, to push them to never give up. The other has the power to tear a person down, to fill them with doubt, to influence them to stop trying. "Yes" and "No".

As adults, it is up to us to encourage our children to never stop dreaming. It is up to us to inspire our children to plant seeds and wish on stars. It is up to us to remind them that it is not about what they see or hear. It is not about how they get around. It is not about what they look like. It is about what they do with the life they have been given.

As an author, educator, and advocate, I am committed to this task. I am committed to being a supporter of those who need support. I am committed to being a cheerleader for the dreamer. I am committed to being a Gardner for the next generation. And I hope you will join me. A part of fulfilling that mission means ensuring that this story, my story, a story for anyone who has ever had a dream, can be accessed by all readers.

If you or someone you love is in need of an accessible copy of "Yes", please visit:

www.frankieannmarcille.com.

Send me a message via the "Contact" tab and I will be in touch to ensure you receive an audio and digital, accessible copy.

Thank you for taking the time to read my story and I wish you the best of luck as you chase your own dreams.

Love always,
Frankie Ann

# Resources

American Printing House for the Blind:
www.aph.org

Perkins eLearning by the Perkins School for the Blind:
www.perkinselearning.org

Braille Institute:
www.brailleinstitute.org

Hadley Vision Resources
www.hadley.edu

Eye.t Assistive Technology Services:
https://eyetvision.com/p/home

The Independent LIttle Bee:
A blog created by Robbin Clarke, Vision Rehabilitation Therapist
and Expanded Core Cirruculum Coordinator for the Utah School for the Deaf and Blind.
http://adifferentkindofvision.blogspot.com/

Camp Abilities:
An international, recreational, adaptive sports camp designed for students
who are blind and visually impaired.
www.campabilities.org
www.campabilitiesworld.com

*In loving memory of Frank Marcille Jr. and Denise Cox.*

CPSIA information can be obtained
at www.ICGtesting.com
Printed in the USA
BVRC102056190721
611885BV00003B/5

* 9 7 8 1 9 5 0 3 2 3 3 8 8 *